THE JUNIOR
DETECTIVE
SERIES

MASTER
OF DISGUISE

by Eugene Baker
illustrated by Lois Axeman

THE
CHILD'S
WORLD

ELGIN, ILLINOIS 60120

Distributed by Childrens Press, 1224 West Van Buren Street, Chicago, Illinois 60607.

Library of Congress Cataloging in Publication Data

Baker, Eugene H
    Master of Disguise.

    (The Junior detective series)
    1. Detectives—Juvenile literature.   2. Imper-
sonation—Juvenile literature.   I. Axeman, Lois.
II. Title.
HV8081.B34   363.2'32   80-11297
ISBN 0-89565-149-1

My name is Dan Darrigan. My partner, Billie-Jo Bravard, and I are Master Detectives. I'm going to share some of our secrets with you. In this book, I will tell you about observing people. We will study disguises, as well.

Observe means "to see." It also means "to pay careful attention." Do you observe with care? What is the color of your teacher's eyes?

A good detective looks at everything. He looks at a person's face, hands, and fingernails. He checks shoes and clothing.

Disguises are also interesting. People can change their looks. They can dress to hide who they are. In this book, you will learn how to disguise yourself.

Observation

Being able to identify someone is necessary in detective work. It helps the police find suspects. It helps in finding missing persons.

Study these people for a minute. Remember that the face and head features are the most important. Also be sure to look at the build, height, and weight. Now, close the book and list five identifying features about each person.

How did you do?

Now, let's study these men together. First, look at their heads. What kind of shapes are they? Is one of them round? Or egg-shaped? Or rectangular? Do any of them have a flat top? Do any of them tilt forward or backward from the body?

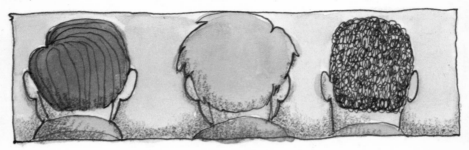

Next, look at the shapes of the faces. Are they long or round, oval or wide?

How about the person's hair? Look at the pictures below. Notice both color and texture. Is the hair blond? Brown? Red? Black? Is it straight? Curly? Wavy? Fuzzy?

Look at the ears. How would you describe them? Are they round or rectangular? Are they pierced? Does the hair cover them? What is the shape of the ear lobe? The ears have the most noticeable features of any part of the head.

Now, study the face. A good plan is to start at the top. How big is the forehead compared to the rest of the face? Are there wrinkles? How does the forehead meet the hairline? Are there any bulges?

Next, check the eyebrows. Do they make an arch or go straight across? Are they bushy or slanted and plucked? Are the eyebrows the same color as the hair?

Look at a person's eyes. Eyes are hard to disguise. Contact lenses can change the color. Notice the color and shape and size of the eyes. Are they round? Oval?

An Oriental person often will have small, almond-shaped eyes. A European's eyes will be large and rounder.

Oriental   European

Everyone's eyes are unique. Does the person squint or blink a great deal? Bloodshot eyes can be an important clue.

Assignment: Ask your teacher,
"What causes bloodshot eyes?"

The nose is another special feature. There are many kinds of noses.

They may be long or short, wide or narrow.

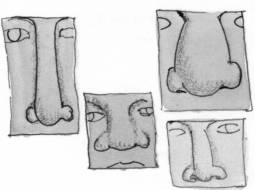

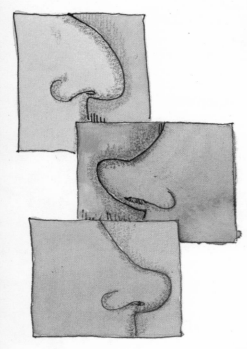

Sometimes they are hooked. They may be tilted. They may have a ball at the end.

An athlete may have a deformed nose. It could have been damaged or broken in a game.

Some people have their noses changed in size or shape by surgery.

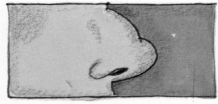

Before   After

How does the mouth look?
Are the lips thick or thin?

Are the lips spread wide? Do
they look like a cupid's bow?

Also notice the teeth. Are
they clean or discolored?

Are there teeth missing, or
are there spaces between the
teeth?

Finally, take an overall look at the face. Are there any face
scars or cuts or blemishes?

If there is a beard or mustache, how does it cover the face?
Is it long or short? Does the color match the hair?

Now it's time to practice. Go to a store or library with a friend. Sit in an out-of-the way place. As people walk by, study their features.

Compare notes with your friend. What did you observe? Keep practicing. You never know when your keen powers to observe will help solve a crime.

Testing Your Powers: Which part of the head has the most noticeable features? (A) Mouth. (B) Shape of Head. (C) Ears. (D) Nose. (E) Neck. (F) Eyes. (See page 6 for the answer.)

Disguises

Sometimes, a detective may need a disguise. When trailing a person, you may want to keep secret who you are. You may need to watch someone closely for days or weeks. Then you will want to look different every day. With practice, you can develop clever disguises. Why, even your best friends will not know you.

Hats

A disguise can be merely a wig and clever make-up. Perhaps a false mustache or beard is enough. Believe it or not, a hat changes how a person looks. It can hide the amount of hair. The hair can be tucked inside the hat and not seen.

Before   After

A hat may make the head seem to be a different shape.

A girl detective can hide her hair under a hat and look like a boy.

A boy detective can attach hair to the inside of a hat and appear to be a girl.

A collection of old hats could be useful to a detective. A hat may be just enough for a disguise some day. Felt hats are the most useful. They can be reshaped. It is easy to trim a felt hat with feathers, ribbons, or colorful cord.

In an emergency, make a hat from cardboard. Pin a strip of paper around your head. Lift it off. It will be in an oval shape.

Using this strip as a pattern, place the oval on a sheet of cardboard. Trace the shape on the cardboard. Draw another oval line one inch inside the first oval. Next, draw a line two or three inches outside the original line, for the brim.

Cut around the outside line. Also cut around the inside line.

Snip through the inside
oval line to the
middle oval line.

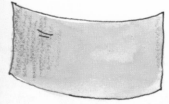

Fold the cardboard up to
make tabs. Later, you can
attach the crown to these tabs.

Then make the crown of the hat.

tall crown

short crown

Staple ends together
to make crown round.

Attach the crown to the
brim. Staple or glue it to the
tabs.

Hair

Hair can be part of an interesting disguise. Often, just changing your own hair will be enough. You can part it on the other side, or in the middle, or not at all.

If you have straight hair, you can curl it.

You can comb your hair or mess it up. You can flatten it with hair spray.

If you have dark hair, you can lighten it. Use powder or stage hair coloring.

If you have light hair, you can darken it. Use eye shadow or stage coloring.

Many colors are available in spray cans. Remember to change the color of your eyebrows, sideburns, and mustache or beard.

Safety Note: Guard your eyes carefully. Don't spray into your face. Never, never try to change the color of your eyelashes.

If your disguise needs a wig, first hide your natural hair. Put on a bathing cap. Or use a stocking cap.

Then you can fasten artificial hair onto a hat.

Add a fringe or braids. Glue them onto the hat.

Wigs help to change how a detective looks. Sometimes, when tailing a suspect, a wig helps.

Sometimes, boys can disguise themselves as girls, by using wigs. And wigs can make girls appear to be boys.

Stretch wigs are often used. They are made of nylon net. They stretch to fit any size head.

Clothes and Shapes

A detective in disguise must wear correct clothes. They help to create the body to go with the disguised face.

Old clothing is often used. Ladies' long evening dresses and men's pajamas can hide the shape of the body. Long underwear can be used.

Often clothes are padded to make a person look heavier. How would you pad yourself?

Decide how you want to look. If you wish to become fatter, use folded sheets or pillows. Wrap them around your middle.

Be sure they are securely pinned.

If you are wearing a coat, get a wooden hanger. Place it upside down across your shoulders in back. This will make you look wider.

One-color clothing makes the shape seem tall.

Different colors and patterns make a shape seem short and wide.

Make-Up

Use make-up to change how your face looks. It will help you feel more like the person you're pretending to be. Make-up also completes the disguise.

Think about the things you learned earlier. Remember that detectives observe people closely.

They note the color of the skin and hair.

They see the wrinkles and lines in the skin.

They study the size and
shape of the hands. . .

the feet. . .

and the head.

They remember these features when they use make-up.

Try to set up a disguise box. Include a variety of make-up items in it. You can use eye shadow on more than eyelids. You can use it under the eyes or under the cheekbones, as well.

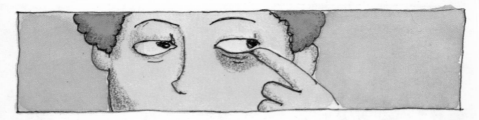

Use lipstick to redden cheeks.

Make-up foundation comes in several colors. Use it as an over-all face color. It can make a person seem pale or sun-tanned.

Pale   Sun-Tanned

The easiest make-up to use is non-greasy. It comes in liquid and in cream.

Cold Cream: Rub on a little cold cream first. It will keep the make-up from sinking into you skin. It is also excellent for removing make-up.

Grease Paint: Grease paint comes in tubes or large crayons. It is available in all shades. Mark strips of grease paint across your face. Spread the color with your fingers.

Nose Putty: Nose putty comes in small sticks. It has many uses. With nose putty, you can change the size of the nose, cover over eyebrows, make the ears stick out. Putty sticks to the skin easily.

Eye Liner and Eyebrow Pencil: These come in several shades. Use them to color around the eyes, to make face lines, and to make face highlights.

Lipstick: It colors the lips. It is useful, as well, to highlight the cheekbones.

New-Skin: This material can make false face scars. Paint a line of new-skin on your face. After it dries, pull the skin around the edges. The skin will pucker around the new-skin. This makes a real-looking scar.

Missing Teeth: You can buy special black grease paint enamel or crayon. Use it to paint over a tooth or teeth. From a distance, the black space looks like a missing tooth.

Create your own make-up box. Practice doing some tricks with make-up. Here are some suggestions.

1. Blend the eye shadow toward the eyebrow. Pencil in a line below the eye that extends beyond the outer edge of the eye. The line will make the eye seem larger.

2. Use nose putty to cover your eyebrows. Then re-draw your eyebrows with black or brown eyebrow pencil. Make them a different shape from your own eyebrows.

3. Blacken several teeth with grease paint enamel. This will make you look older.

4. Draw animal scratches on the skin with lipstick or fingernail polish.

5. Create old scars and bruised spots with dark lipstick and eyebrow pencil.

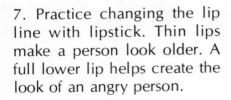

6. Lighten the eyebrows and draw shadows under your eyes with grey eye liner. Use grey eye shadow on cheeks. This will make them look sunken and hollow.

7. Practice changing the lip line with lipstick. Thin lips make a person look older. A full lower lip helps create the look of an angry person.

8. Use make-up to make yourself look different. If your eyes are small, make them seem larger. Change the look of your nose or your mouth.

Final Assignment

Let's say you decide to disguise yourself as an old man. First, decide whether to be a grumpy old man or a kindly, grandfather type.

Spread a pale make-up foundation all over your face, neck, and hands.

Look in a mirror and frown. Use an eyebrow pencil to fill in at least three of these frown lines on your forehead.

Now squint your eyes. Take the eyebrow pencil and mark the "crow's feet" lines on the outer corners of the eyes.

Make grey shadows under the eyes.

Powder or color your eyebrows.

Suck in your cheeks. Where the hollows appear, darken with make-up.

Use a beige bathing cap to appear bald. Pull some hair out at the sides.

Glue extra hair to the sides of the cap.

Color the hair white by patting white powder on it.

Now, glue on a white beard.

Decide if you wish the hair to appear wild and scraggly or natty and trim. Cut and comb the hair and beard, to get the look you want.

Add a pair of wire-rimmed glasses. Wear them low on your nose.

Then, put padding on your back, between your shoulders.

Old people walk huddled over. They may walk slowly, with a cane.

Say, you look great! You're ready for any detective assignment that requires a disguise. You could use that disguise as a Halloween costume, as well.

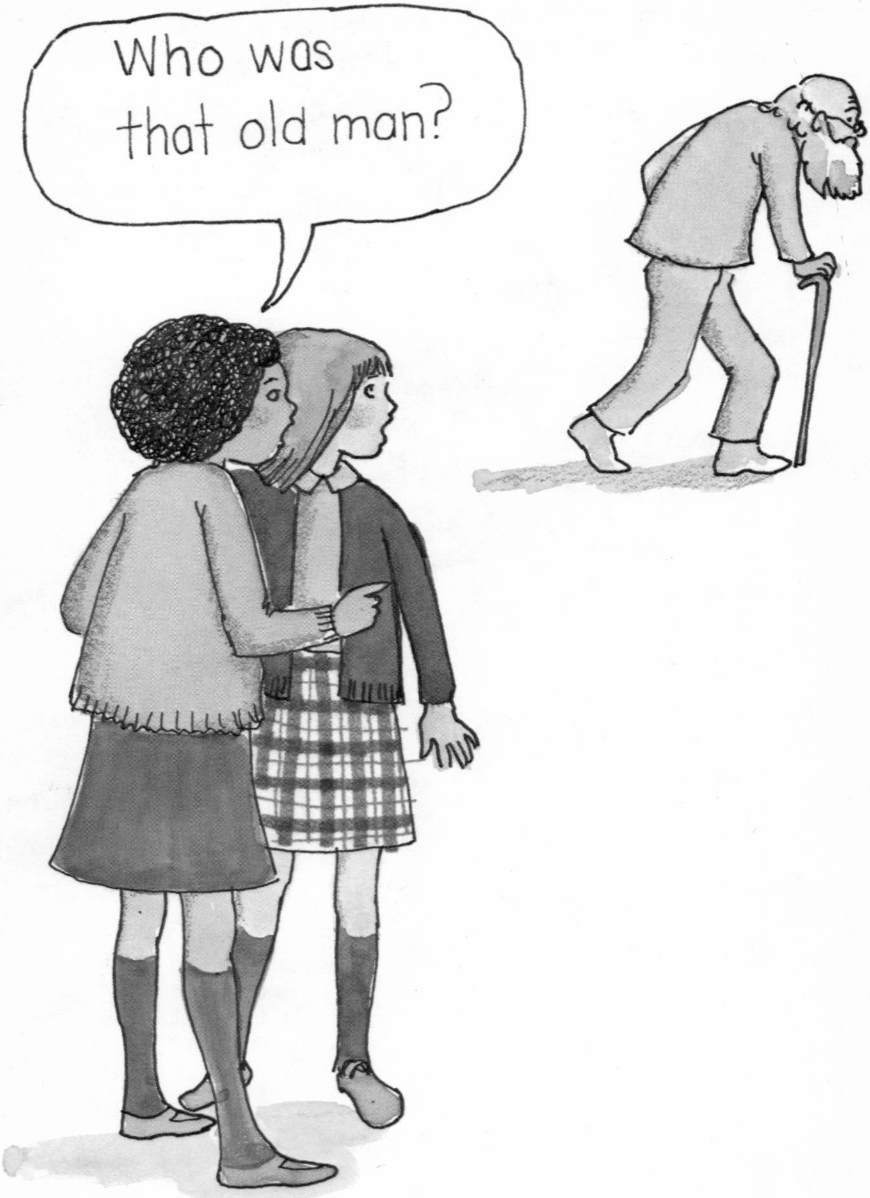
Who was
that old man?